This book belongs to

Provenance

Scotland's folklore has many stories about fairies. Music, lost time and bargaining with fairies are common elements. *The Fairy Song* draws particularly on 'The Tramp and the Boots' as told by Scottish Traveller Duncan Williamson in *The Coming of the Unicorn*, edited by Linda Williamson (Floris Books), and on 'The Humph at the Fit o the Glen and the Humph at the Heid o the Glen' from *The Last of the Tinsmiths: The Life of Willie MacPhee*, edited by Sheila Douglas (Birlinn).

'I Dream'd I Lay' is a song by Scotland's favourite poet, Robert Burns.

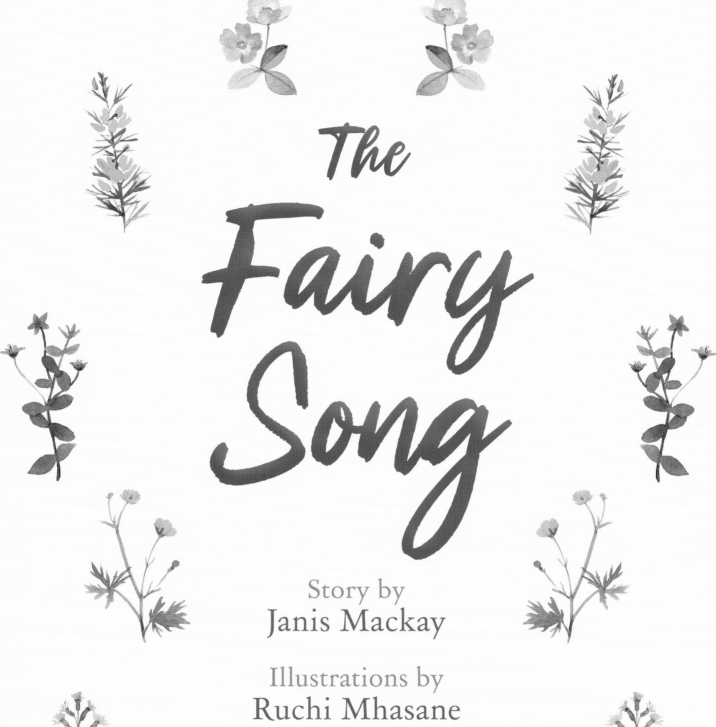

The
Fairy
Song

Story by
Janis Mackay

Illustrations by
Ruchi Mhasane

TRADITIONAL SCOTTISH TALES

Rose lived with her parents in a small house in the forest.
From dawn to dusk the three cut wood and collected
sticks to sell at market. They were very poor.

Rose longed for laughter and play, and she loved roses – the flowers that shared her name. But her parents were so worried about earning enough money for food that they couldn't think about anything else.

When neighbouring children came to the house, Rose's father sent them away. "There's no time for play, Rose has sticks to bundle," he said.

And when Rose asked if she could clear a patch of ground to plant wild roses, her mother said, "Rose, my darling lass, we can't eat flowers."

Rose's father carried wood to market every weekday, and on Saturdays Rose made the long walk to sell her bundles of sticks. Her boots were broken and their soles were so thin every pebble on the path hurt her feet. Rose had a lovely voice, and to keep her mind off the soreness, she would sing as she walked:

I dream'd I lay
Where flowers were springing
Gaily in the sunny beam;
List'ning to
The wild birds singing,
By a falling crystal stream...

One year, Midsummer's Day fell on a Saturday. Rose was trudging home wearily after market, singing, when she heard someone else singing too. The voice sounded like bells tinkling. Rose followed the beautiful music through the forest.

Breathless, she came to a small
grassy hill in a clearing. The singing
was coming from under the hill!

Rose lay down and pressed her ear to the mossy grass.
She had never heard such wondrous music.
Buttercup and pimpernel, rang out the joyful song.
Then again, Buttercup and pimpernel...

The ground seemed to tremble.
Rose sat up in wonder as a tiny door opened
in the grass. From it shone rays of coloured light.
Little winged children came streaming out
of the hill! They skipped, flitted and
twirled into the bright midsummer
air. Wide-eyed, Rose stared.
These were surely fairies!

Buttercup and pimpernel... the fairies sang.
Buttercup and pimpernel...
Buttercup and pimpernel...

Though the singing was lovely, Rose grew tired of the same words, over and over. She waited for a pause in the tune. Then in her clear voice she sang out:

"*...And wild roses too!*"

The fairies froze in mid-air, then spun to glare at her, as though they were only now really noticing her. Their sweet singing ceased, and they scowled.

Rose gasped as the frowning fairies flew at her!

But then one fairy, a beautiful buttercup fairy, darted swiftly in front of the others. Her shimmering wings fluttered as she landed lightly on Rose's hand, and smiled.

"Thank you," the fairy murmured, "for giving us a new line for our midsummer song."

Buttercup and pimpernel

she softly sang, then added,

and wild roses too...

One by one the other fairies joined in:

and wild roses too!

"What is your name, child?" asked the buttercup fairy.

"Rose," Rose replied.

"You have a fairy name!" trilled the fairy. "Stay and dance," she continued, "we're having a midsummer party!"

The fairies placed a garland of wild summer flowers on Rose's head.

Rose laughed. "Like a queen!" she said, kicking off her broken boots and spinning around. "Oh, I'll stay for a wee while then." She knew her parents were waiting. "Just for two dances."

Rose twirled, birled and sang with the
fairies on the fairy hill. Never in her life
had she felt so glad and free.

Buttercup and pimpernel.

The midsummer song soared on and on.

And wild roses too!

Leaping and laughing, Rose tripped on her old boots. "Oh!" she cried, surprised by them.

Sighing, she bent to put them on. She had surely finished her two dances by now.

"Stay with us," begged the dancing fairies, "forever."

The word shocked Rose. She thought again of her waiting parents.

"You belong with us, Rose-with-the-fairy-name, Rose-with-the-beautiful-singing," chanted the fairies.

"I must get home! Please let me go." Rose's thoughts whirled. What could she offer them? "I'll— I'll plant roses in the forest to bloom every midsummer," she tried.

"Yes, do!" called the buttercup fairy. "We'll miss you, wild Rose!"

The singing faded. Rose sat up on the grassy hill.

The fairies had disappeared.

Perhaps the song was always just the birds trilling, and the trickle of water nearby? Perhaps the fairies had been a dream?

But then Rose gasped for joy. On her feet, instead of her broken boots, were the most exquisite, soft shoes.

"Thank you," she whispered to the hill.

In no time she found the path, and skipped in her beautiful shoes through fallen leaves all the way home.

As she ran up to the house, Rose's parents stared, amazed. They burst into tears of joy.

"We thought you were lost!" they cried.

Her mother wept. "You left us at midsummer and now it is autumn. Oh, where have you been, my dear, dear child?"

Rose looked around and saw the brambles were ripe on the thorns. The birch trees had shed their leaves and the old oak had turned yellow.

"I have been with the fairies," she said. "But… it was just two dances!"

Her parents hugged her tightly.

From that time, it seemed to Rose that the days were brighter. Her parents agreed she could play with the neighbouring children after she had collected her sticks. Her mother and father loved to hear her sing. And her friends helped her plant wild roses, just as she had promised the fairies.

The roses flourished, and Rose took bunches to market, where people came from near and far to buy them.

Her beautiful fairy shoes never wore out, and as Rose grew, the shoes grew with her.

Though she tried again to find the fairy hill, she never could.

But Rose never forgot the fairies, or their song.

And one Midsummer's Day, years later, when she was tending her flowers in the forest, she heard music a long, long way off. She stopped and listened to a sound like faint tinkling bells on the gentle breeze:

Buttercup and pimpernel...

Buttercup and pimpernel...

Buttercup and pimpernel... And wild roses too.

To Friha – may flowers grow,
and to David Campbell – thank you for the stories
– J.M.

For the special ones who have walked with me in forests,
and stopped to look at the magic of flowers
– R.M.

The illustrations in this book were created using pencil and watercolour, and were finished digitally.

Kelpies is an imprint of Floris Books. First published in 2021 by Floris Books. Text © 2021 Janis Mackay. Illustrations © 2021 Ruchi Mhasane
Janis Mackay and Ruchi Mhasane assert their right under the Copyright, Designs and Patent Act 1988 to be recognised as the Author and
Illustrator of this Work. All rights reserved. No part of this book may be reproduced without the prior permission of Floris Books, Edinburgh
www.florisbooks.co.uk British Library CIP data available. ISBN 978-178250-747-5 Printed in China through Asia Pacific Offset

FSC
www.fsc.org
MIX
Paper from
responsible sources
FSC® C012521

Floris Books supports sustainable forest management
by printing this book on materials made from wood that
comes from responsible sources and reclaimed material